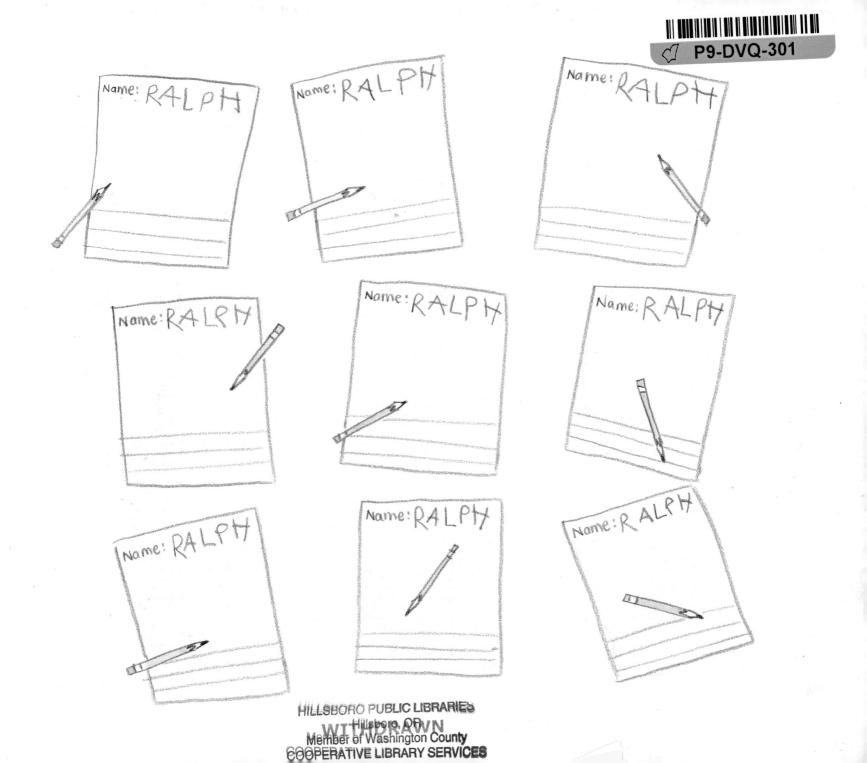

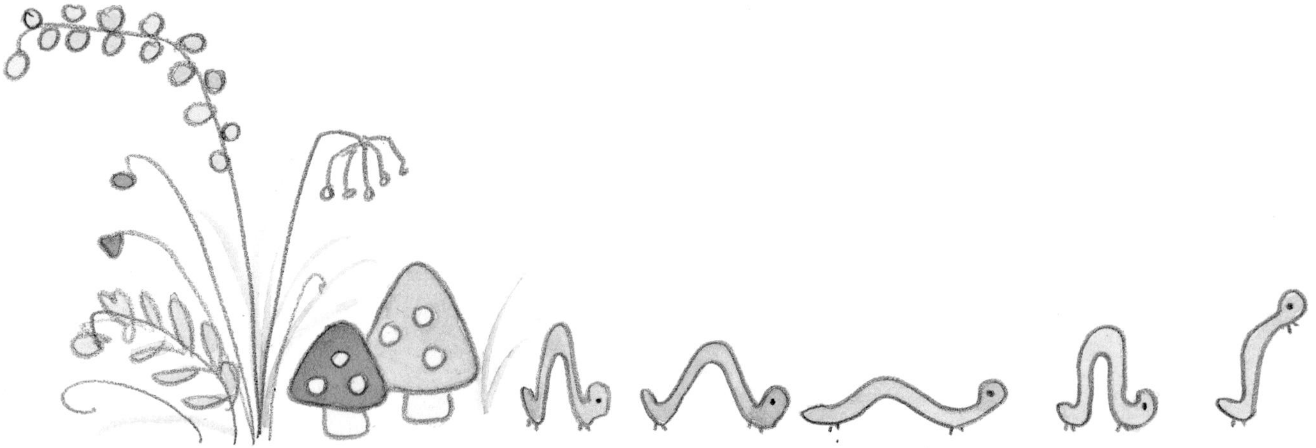

Ralph Tells a Story
by Abby Hanlon

Amazon Children's Publishing

Amazon Publishing

Attn: Amazon Children's Books

P.O. Box 400818

Las Vegas, NV, 89149

www.amazon.com/amazonchildrenspublishing

Library of Congress Cataloging-in-Publication Data

Hanlon, Abby.

Ralph tells a story / by Abby Hanlon. — 1st ed.

p. cm.

Summary: Although his teacher insists there are stories everywhere, Ralph cannot think of any to write.

ISBN 978-0-7614-6180-7 (hardcover) — ISBN 978-0-7614-6182-1 (ebook)

[1. Creative writing—Fiction. 2. Schools—Fiction.] I. Title.

PZ7.H196359Ral 2012

[E]—dc23

2011036608

5039 8808 1/13

The illustrations are rendered in watercolor and colored pencil.

Book design by Anahid Hamparian

Editor: Marilyn Brigham

Printed in China (W)

First edition

10 9 8 7 6 5 4 3 2 1

For Lulu, Burke, and Nicky

My teacher always said,

"Stories are everywhere!"

And the kids in my class were always finding them.

But every day at writing time,

I thought really hard.   I stared at my paper.   I stared at the ceiling.

I could not write a story.

So I looked for other things to do.

I went to the water fountain.

I roamed the hallways.

I tried everything.

Then one day, after getting sent back to my desk, I begged Daisy for help. "I can't write a story because NOTHING happens to me!"

"Are you kidding?" she said. "I've written a ton of stories about you!"

She began pulling her stories out of her desk. "Look at this one," she said. "Remember the time you let me brush your hair? And this one! Remember the time you knocked down all the crayons? Oh and remember the time you painted your nails with a black marker?"

I thought, *I'll never be a great writer like Daisy.*

Then Daisy stapled all her stories together. *Click click!* "Wow!" she said. "This book is already thirteen pages!" *Click click!*

"Can I use the stapler?" I asked. I was *really* good at stapling. "But you have nothing to staple!" said Daisy. "You have to find a story first!"

So I looked for stories
out the window . . .

in the aquarium . . .

. . . in my desk.

And when my teacher wasn't looking,
I looked for stories on the floor.

But still no stories.

Lying under my desk reminded me of lying in the grass at the park. I closed my eyes and imagined I was at the park . . . just like that time a little inchworm crawled on my knee. The sun was shining right into my eyes. Squinting, I picked up the wiggly inchworm and looked at it close-up.

And that's when my teacher found me. "What's your story about?" she asked.

I opened my eyes. "Um . . . um . . . I saw an inchworm."

"Wonderful!" she said. "I can't wait to read what you wrote."

But there was no inchworm story!

I sat down and tried to write about the inchworm, but right away I got stuck.

"Do you know any inchworm stories?" I asked Daisy. She just rolled her eyes and kept on writing.

And then my teacher said:

"Ralph, why don't you go first?" said the teacher.
I pretended that I had lost my paper.

It didn't work.

I walked to the front of
the rug. It took a long time.

I held my paper against my
chest so no one could see it.
"I was at the park," I said.
"An inchworm crawled on
my knee."

It was quiet.

My heart went: *Thump. Thump. Thump. Thump.*

That's when I looked at Daisy.

And then everybody started asking me questions.

Wait a minute! I thought. SOMETHING DID HAPPEN WITH THAT INCHWORM!

Everybody clapped and cheered. "Show the picture, Ralph," someone said.

I wasn't embarrassed anymore so I did.

That was last year. This year I write stories all the time. I keep finding stories everywhere.

Writing Tips from Ralph

Books by Ralph

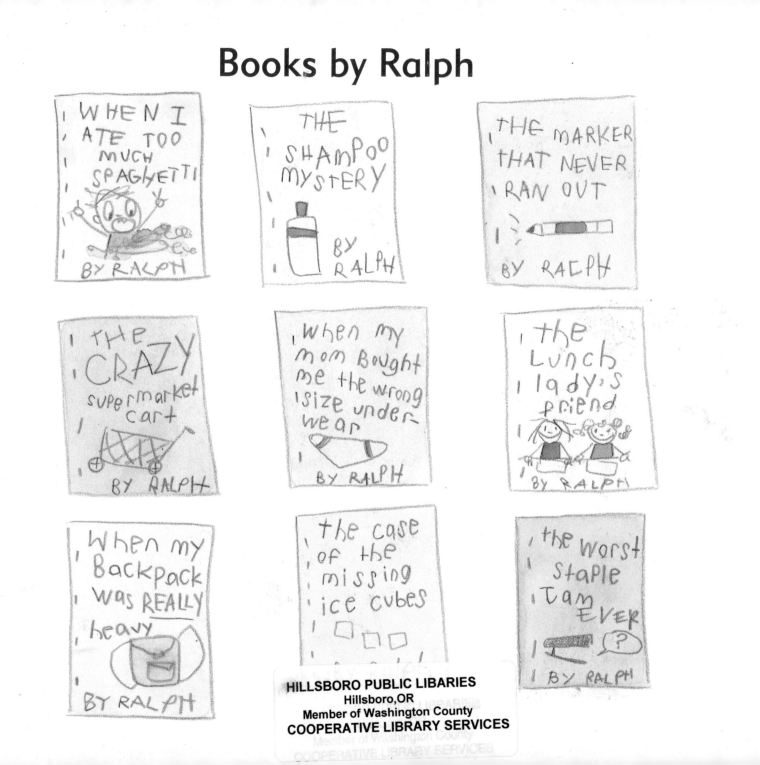